Lin City Stories

This collection is dedicated to my Mom,
who has always pushed me to be the best
I can be, and my Dad, who is the most
truthful and dedicated editor I know.

Table of Contents

The Call from Below

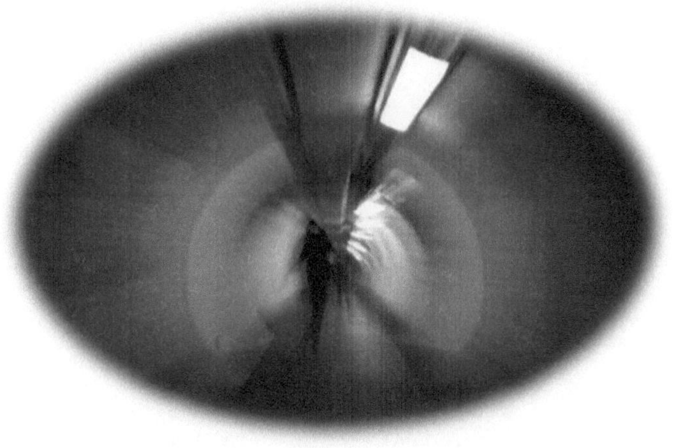

Scene 1: The Call

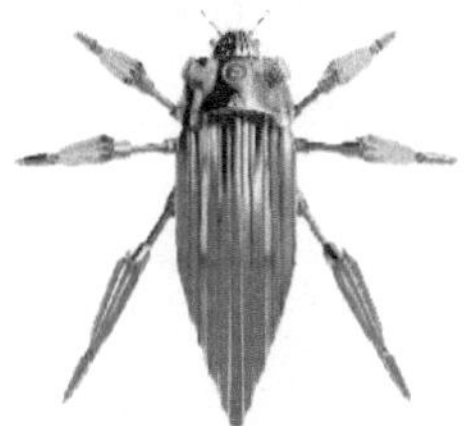

It was 8:00 A.M. when I received the call.

It was 8:00 A.M. when my life changed forever.

Everything started normally. I had been called to work early. We had scheduled routine maintenance on the NanoTech computers and I needed to ensure that all of Mr. Anderson's files were intact. I loved coming in early to Nanotech. Lin City was still dark, and the speakers that usually emitted sounds of birds now filled the air with the calming chirp of crickets. The city was still, and the smell of street-cleaning solution filled the air with the scent of imitation lemon.

I arrived at the building while the night cleaning crew was leaving, and I walked to my office in silence. I brushed my hand against the smooth marble railing as I climbed the plush stairs, taking in the grandeur of the building. It had magnificent architecture combined with sleek materials a masterpiece. Whenever I entered Nanotech, I knew it was exactly where I belonged.

My office was as I had left it the day before, with shining white floors and crystal-clear windows that stretched the entire height of the room. I had suggested adding some color to the room. My request had been denied. Not good for productivity. Mr. Anderson was very particular about his suite and preferred that the cleaning crew avoid his office and adjacent rooms for fear of them misplacing a tablet that had been left out. I always thought this was strange because I never left a tablet out, but I also never argued.

I began my work, double and triple checking that each and every one of Mr. Anderson's files was in the right place. Usually, I could become completely engrossed in my work, but that day, I felt *off.* With a quick scan of the room, I realized that nothing was physically out of place. It was something in the air.

That's when I got the call.

The line number looked like it had originated from a lower level of the city, but it was easy to mistake different levels' numbers at a quick glance. I opened the call quickly and spoke into my earpiece, you should never leave someone on the other line for too long; that was one the first things Mr. Anderson had ever taught me.

"Hello! This is Ms. Stao at Nanotech Incorporated, how may I assist you?" I asked.

The caller breathed loudly, something I detested.

"Hello?" I spoke again, louder this time.

"Have you seen the belly of the beast?"

The silence following the question was like a herd of elephants. The caller sounded like they would continue, but I wouldn't let them. I couldn't let them. I had gotten strange calls before, but none that made my stomach drop like this one had.

"Thank you for your call, have a pleasant day." I said as calmly as I could.

I had known fake calls were part of the job description, but they still concerned me whenever the office received one. Every time I got a call like this, it was hard to get back to work; it felt like someone was watching me. Of course, someone was watching me, there were security cameras everywhere.

I left my office and walked around the perimeter of Nanotech to calm my mind. The silence of the city and the blue skies of the upper levels were always able to comfort me when I was stressed about work, I could actually hear myself think outside, without the quiet buzz of technology in my office. I don't know how I would ever think if I had to listen to even more noise all day.

When Nanotech moved its headquarters to Lin City, the company made some changes. All of the residents of Uptown, and some of the middle levels, were required to wrap all household appliances with a thick, sound-dampening foam that absorbed any sound they made. Lights in the lower city (Downtown) and factories were swapped for blue. The lack of sunlight in the lower levels made it so the blue lights obscured almost every color. Noiseless trams had been installed throughout Uptown, and any transportation other than foot traffic was made impossible by the web of catwalks and scaffolding in the rest of the city.

Those changes were made forty-five years ago, and now the city is even more polished. It has been made a pinnacle for the rest of the world. I am part of that pinnacle.

I returned to my office after walking to find that Mr. Anderson had already begun working in his suite, and a stack of new files was waiting for me. Usually, I was happy to have work waiting for me, I could dive in and forget about the outside world for a few hours. Instead, I tracked the origin of the call through my console. I suppose someone could blame something like this on human curiosity, but the tug in my gut felt stronger than human nature. I was right that it had been a Downtown number and an old one at that. Numbers tied to a specific place were only issued in special cases. I switched the address coordinates to my datapad and walked out of the building. Everyone trusted that I was going somewhere important, and they didn't try to stop me.

My parents made it easy for me to go wherever I wanted. My father had worked closely with Mr. Anderson when they were younger. They were the reason that NanoTech was where it was today. That was why, when I lost my vision as a child, I received an intraocular implant and nanobot treatments. Once I was old enough to work, Mr. Anderson was more than happy to hire me as his assistant. No one had questioned me before I began working, and they were even less likely to now.

I walked past the tram station and arrived at a large white gate, the entrance to the lower sections of the city. You didn't need your identification to get into the lower levels, you only needed it to get back up.

I began my trek down the cascading waterfall of sidewalks, passing other Uptown citizens there on business, and some Downtown workers on their mandatory breaks. My parents had told me that they got too many breaks, if I was able to work all day, surely they were as well, right? I finally reached the coordinates in the seventh level of the city. There was no light except for the blue bulbs on every store and house porch. The address led me to a blue-washed convenience store with a blue OPEN sign illuminating the front step. A single use datapad was next to the front step, and the start-up screen had my name on it.

I looked around the street and saw workers quickly approaching with clear plastic lunch bags, so I stashed the tablet in my jacket. I walked back to the upper city, resisting the urge to run when I saw someone look in my direction. Some may say I was over-cautious, but I was terrified of being caught with an unauthorized datapad. When I arrived in Uptown, I scanned my ID badge and entered my apartment.

I opened the tablet at my desk, and when it asked for a fingerprint, it recognized mine as the owner.

Hello Aria, We hope this message finds you well. cahoNnet nadpecrrolto is not what it seems. You must find the belly of the beast. The safety of Lin City rests in your hands alone. Level 2 299.

The caller's phrase, "the belly of the beast," rang in my head from my previous encounter with the term. I recognized the last part of the message as an address, one that was on a lower level than I had ever been.

There were a total of twelve levels in the city. I had gone down to Level Seven today when I was tracking the call, and that was the lowest I had ever explored. Most people on Level Seven worked as low-level managers who traveled around the city, or were people of my station visiting for meetings. Level Two was different. Those living on Level Two were factory workers and manual laborers. Many of them had never seen the sun and would never see it.

Pictures of Downtown weren't often shown to those in Uptown, so I had never even seen what it was like. I had heard about it, though, and that affirmed my decision to never visit. But it looked like I would need to go now if I ever wanted to find out what was happening.

The next day, I did just that.

Scene 2: The Search

I woke up earlier than normal and called in sick to work. I swapped my blue uniform for common clothing and ate a breakfast of nutrient packs before leaving my apartment. The view of the sky from the twelfth level was still black and the lights from the lower city shone up through spaces between the various platforms. I found a recycling unit and wiped the datapad I had found on Seven, leaving it to be used for another, hopefully less creepy, purpose. I left the upper city by way of a vertical tram; I couldn't risk anyone seeing me walk down. The tram only traveled to Level Five, and I had to walk the rest of the way. I kept my head covered with my dark coat whenever I passed someone, which in hindsight, probably made me look more suspicious than I intended.

I held my personal datapad in my hand and looked for the address on every door on Level Two. The smell was disturbing, and I wanted to go back to my cozy apartment as fast as I could. I heard a strange sound and stopped. Only for a second, but it was long enough. A figure sat huddled on the steps of a run-down house, staring at me with large, tear-filled eyes. They stood like they were going to approach me.

I turned and walked faster down the street. I couldn't stop for anyone, no matter what. My parents always told me I shouldn't feel sorry for those on lower levels. If they had worked harder, they would be successful like we were. Their words didn't stop the twinge of guilt I felt whenever I saw someone asleep on the corner or digging in the waste food collectors.

I had expected the people on levels as low as this to be aggressive and dangerous, but I guessed the blue light prevented that. The lights had been installed to keep people calm and focused. Nanotech wanted their workers to be productive, but these people just looked dejected and sleep deprived.

When I found 299, I sighed in relief. It was another convenience store, the same company as before. I looked around but found no datapad this time, only another blue sign that read OPEN. With no better ideas, I stepped inside. The lights outside gave everything a blue tone, and the labels on packaged meals were barely legible.

I took a lap around the store, looking for hidden signs as I reread the message from my pad.

cahoNnet nadpecrroIto

I had looked everywhere in the store, scanned every shelf, and found nothing. I clenched my fist in frustration and grabbed a can off a nearby shelf, ready to throw it at the concrete floor. But I stopped.

In my hand I held a can that read; "cahoNnet nadpecrroIto The Best Shelf Fruit for You and Me!" I twisted the can in my hand.

The can looked like all the others on the shelf, a dark blue package with a stylized picture of tropical fruit in bold colors, But the name of the product had been edited on this one. I shoved the can in my bag and left the store, ignoring the calls of the shop-runner. I couldn't let anyone see this can.

I ran up through the city and found refuge behind a meal station on Level Five. I pulled the package out of my bag and opened it like an animal, ignoring the plastic that cut my hands. Inside the mangled package was a small chip the size of a pea. I inspected the chip between my fingers. It was metal and covered with intricately placed gold wires.

I shook the rest of the contents of the package out into my hand, and besides a few pieces of dry fruit, there was a note written on plain paper. Paper was expensive in the city, as almost everyone used datapads when they needed to write anything. The note only had two words.

Mari Nev

It was a name, and I knew who it belonged to. Mari Nev had worked as a doctor in the lower levels of Lin City before being charged with performing illegal cosmetic surgeries. Turning people into animal-like creatures and putting patients under his knife to perform unimaginable experiments. And I needed to find him.

I grabbed a booth in an automated diner and began my search, starting with broad terms on my datapad. I found hundreds of news and tabloid pieces about the doctor's various scandals, court cases, and victims. It seemed like journalists had been tripping over themselves to find the location of his next secret lab or photographs of his experiments. When I finally found an article about his capture, I was surprised. Mari Nev had not been executed like most dangerous criminals were. He was still in Lin City.

Scene 3: The Prisoner

I stayed overnight on the seventh level. I was too likely to see someone I knew any higher. I called Nanotech employee security to inform them that I would be out sick for a second day, and though they sounded skeptical, they were smart enough not to question me. I knew it would be dangerous for my parents if I were caught outside of work, and it was better if I pretended I couldn't go at all.

Dr. Nev had been imprisoned on the lowest level of the city, the one reserved for criminals alone. You needed incredibly high clearance codes to access the level. Lucky for me, being the Executive Assistant to the highest-ranking official of Nanotech came with some perks.

I told the guards at the front gate that Mr. Anderson required certain information about a prisoner, and that I was sent to collect it personally. I expected a barrage of questions, but with a flash of my Nanotech ID, a guard led me into the city's high security prison.

Dr. Nev was kept in a dark corner of the vast building, at the end of a long line of cells made by green electric fields. Other prisoners looked at me as I passed.

Some begged for food, only to be met by an electric shock from the walls of their cell.

The guard accompanying me gestured to Dr. Nev's cell. There was a fingerprint pad and a cell number on the outside of the cell. I could barely see the occupant until I stood directly in front of the door.

"I need to speak privately with Dr. Nev. I will let you know if I require assistance." The guard looked at me for a moment before walking back towards the entrance to the hall. I turned to the doctor.

"Dr. Nev," I pulled the chip out from my pocket. "Do you know what this is?"

The electric field shimmered as the man in the corner approached. He was thin, no doubt as a result of the prison diet, and stood hunched, with long white hair tied in braids and deeply wrinkled skin. A look of recognition darted through his eyes.

"Where did you get that?"

"Doctor, do you know what this is? My employer and I find this information extremely valuable."

The Doctor looked at me, stony eyes meeting mine.

"Yes, I know what it is. It's a storage chip for a B12 intraocular implant. The B12 model was only used for a few years before they locked me up here. What I don't know is why you have it."

The B12 model. The same one that restored my vision as a child.

I was confused, and it showed in my voice "I found it, and I think it was left for me to find. It was left next to a note with your name on it. Why?"

"Perhaps because I'm the only doctor who knows the procedure required to implant that device who isn't currently employed with Nanotech. And if my suspicions are correct, I'm the one who made that chip."

I was surprised that someone outside of Nanotech had gotten their hands on this kind of advanced technology, but I had known Nev was skeevy since the first time I had read his name.

"How did you get Nanotech technology?" I asked.

The doctor laughed for an uncomfortably long time before answering. "You poor, naive girl. Nanotech is not the only intelligent group in the city. If you trust me, you will be able to see so much more. You will see the truth about it all."

"How can I see the information?" I asked, "If it's a data chip, there must be somewhere I can view it."

I was picturing something like a special datapad port, or a computer in the upper city. The truth was much more gruesome.

"Unless you have access to a programming unit, the only way to view the information is to connect the data chip directly to a B12 implant. No shortcuts, I'm afraid."

I turned away from the grinning doctor, "If, hypothetically, I did want the surgery, what would you want in exchange?"

"You get me out of here, and I'll do it. But I won't be coming back after we're done."

I called the guard back to the cell. "I am going to give you money now, and you are going to let this man come with me."

I showed the guard a fund transfer waiting to be confirmed on my datapad. His eyes lit up, but I could see hesitation in how his hand rested on his weapon.

"If you don't let this man walk out with me," I went on, "I may have to report an incident to my supervisor,

Mr. Anderson." The guard's eyes widened before he scrambled to the pin pad next to the cell, not even checking to see if the transfer had happened before scurrying away from me and the doctor. Some might say my method was too direct, but I didn't want to waste time with pleasantries.

The doctor stepped out of the cell, holding onto my arm for balance. He shook like a leaf in the wind, making my own legs unsteady. His pale, bony fingers wrapped around my wrist and I could feel his jagged fingernails cutting through my jacket. I held him up, but his physical condition was worrying. I had read that he was incarcerated when he was fifty-three, and twenty years later, he resembled a ninety-year-old.

"Are you positive you will be able to perform the procedure?" My voice wavered, but I quickly corrected it.

Mari Nev was not someone to whom you wanted to show fear.

"My legs may be weak, but my hands are as steady as ever," he said. "I will perform the surgery."

Dr. Nev followed me from the building, guards watching us closely every step we took. The only way out of Level One was by armed escort, and as we made our way back to Level Two, the officers trailing us did nothing to prevent the stares I had predicted we would see. Nev had been incarcerated so long ago that he was nearly unrecognizable.

I rented a basement from a family on the sixth level. I wanted to apologize for what would take place in their home but held my tongue. I stayed in the small living room to sleep and advised Dr. Nev to do the same, but when I woke only twenty minutes later, the doctor was walking through the basement door with bags full of medical equipment. The dining table was sterilized with a glowing device that shed light throughout the entire room, and the doctor laid out a series of implements on a small tray next to the table. Dr. Nev donned a mask and mismatched latex gloves. It was hard to tell behind the mask, but I could've sworn he was smiling as he wiggled his fingers into the gloves.

As I stood next to the table, a flood of anxiety rushed through me. What was I even doing? Was I going insane?

"What's on the chip anyway? Why do I need to see it?"

The doctor held the chip to the light "If I am correct, this chip has sensitive and important information. I believe I know what organization left it for you to find." He spoke matter-of-factly, like I hadn't just helped him escape from prison, or that we weren't about to perform surgery on my eye.

"What organization?" I had never heard of any groups besides Nanotech having access to this kind of technology.

"With the information on this, you will find out soon enough."

I didn't trust Dr. Nev, but I did trust that whatever was on this chip would change everything.

"Let's do it."

Scene 4: The Truth

I came to with Dr. Nev leaning over me wearing his surgical gear and giving me a thumbs up, a strange sight to see as you woke up from a medical procedure.

"The surgery was a success. Your implant should be receiving the data shortly."

I looked around and blinked spots from my eyes.

Text scrolled across my vision so quickly that I could barely read it. Pictures flashed in front of me. Pictures of me, pictures of the different levels of the city, and some pictures of people I had never seen before. I narrated everything to the doctor as fast as I could and he typed it all into my datapad. And then it was over. Just as fast as the information had appeared, it was gone.

I remembered a similar flash of information from when I had first received the implant, but it had just been codes and numbers. This time was like seeing a lifetime of memories-flash before my eyes, but the life was someone else's.

"What was that? Who were those people?" I sat up and faced the doctor, reading over his transcribed notes.

"Those are members of cahoNnet. An underground organization in Lin City. Their goal is to uncover the less-tasteful acts of Nanotech." The doctor spoke quickly as he dumped his mask and gloves into the apartment's trash receptacle.

I recalled the pictures of myself in the data stream, wearing my work uniform and speaking into my earpiece from my desk. "Why were there pictures of me on there? I've never even heard of this group, and I'm most definitely not part of it."

The doctor laughed, "Aria, you have been a part of this ever since you got that call."

I looked back at my datapad. What I had been reciting wasn't just gibberish. I had been reading names, dates, addresses, phone numbers, and security codes. When I looked up to the doctor, to plead for information, he was gone.

I stumbled out of the basement onto the street, where was I supposed to go now? The sky had grown dark and the unfamiliar shadows seemed to reach towards me. What was I supposed to do? I found my way to one of the addresses that was on the datapad. The doctor must have been right about creating this before his incarceration; the building that the address belonged to was nowhere in sight, just an empty alleyway. I leaned against the side of the alley and put my head against the wall in frustration. There had been no instructions given, just information. I had come all this way, for what? If this organization wanted me to save Lin City, they couldn't just abandon me. I leaned my head against the wall and another flash of information appeared. This time, it was about Nanotech.

I fumbled with my datapad and began typing everything as fast as I could. After the morbid adventures of the past few days, words popping into my vision were unsurprising. I tried to capture the images I saw in words. I must've looked insane, rubbing my head against the wall in an effort to retrieve as much information as possible. When the stream stopped this time, I knew it was truly the end. Blood dripped down my face and left a wet residue on the wall, but the information in front of me was more gruesome than any blood stain in an alley.

Nanotech has been using its creations, its Nanobots, for unimaginable reasons. Super-human forces were being created by flooding unsuspecting victims looking for treatment with Nanobots and hijacking their minds to make it seem like they were their normal selves while being controlled from the inside. World leaders had been killed by the Nanobots, leaving Nanotech in control of their citizens. Images showed my own father standing beside prison cells holding hijacked soldiers.

I slid to the ground, wiping blood and tears from my eyes. Everything I had ever thought I had known was a lie. I had dedicated years of my life to a company that was killing its own people in twisted experiments. Opposing Nanotech scared me but knowing that I was a part of it scared me even more.

At the end of the data stream, there was a message:

You have seen the belly of the beast.

You now must expose it.

I left the alleyway, ignoring the people who stared as I walked past them. I made my way up the levels, disregarding my earlier need for caution. Some asked me if I needed help, but I brushed them aside. I had to go up. I rode the vertical tram back to Level Eleven, already pulling out my ID as I approached the white gate that marked the entrance to Level Twelve. I must have been quite the sight. My eye had been bruised by the surgery and my forehead was covered in scrapes. The guard at the gate stopped me with an outstretched hand and asked for my ID.

I wondered if this was one of the guards hijacked with Nanobots. His expression seemed normal, uninterested. I held out my ID and studied him as I passed. I caught a glimpse of skin through his uniform and saw a long scar running horizontally along the base of his head, similar to that of some of the pictures I had seen through the implant. I shuddered to imagine being controlled like that. To have no free will at all was a terrifying thought. I may have been lied to, but at least I had the chance to learn the truth. And now I would make it so everyone else could too.

I covered my face with my ID card as I entered my apartment building. I didn't want word to get back to my parents about how I had presented myself in public. They were the first people I thought to tell when I learned of Nanotech's betrayal, but of course they already knew. After working within the heart of Nanotech, my parents must have witnessed the torture of innocent people, even encouraged it. Anything to make their lives easier. Anything to make my life easier.

My hand shook as I used my ID on my apartment door. It pushed inward and I collapsed against the kitchen table, sobbing. I grabbed a vase from my table and hurled it at the wall. The faux glass exploded across the room. *How could I have benefited from the suffering of others for so long? How could these people who have known me all my life hide something like this from me?* The glass snapped as I walked over it, leaving a trail of fine powder in my wake.

I donned my light blue work uniform, tying my hair into a tight round bun. I was able to cover what injuries my first aid kit couldn't fix with makeup. I packed a bag for work with my datapad and a light snack, just in case I managed to survive the day.

It felt strange to walk across Uptown like everything was normal. The hidden speakers played exotic bird calls accompanied by the sound of a babbling brook, and the rising sun told me I had stayed up all night getting ready for my mission that day. I had gone through every possibility in my mind and there was only one option, only one way to free Lin City. The Nanotech tower loomed above me like an ancient tree waiting to burn, and the matches were sitting in my bag.

People greeted me at the entrance like I had never been gone, asking how my parents were, and congratulating me on the raise they assumed I was getting soon. How many of these people knew what was really going on in Nanotech? Were they like me, just as deceived and ignorant? I tried to assume that they knew nothing as we exchanged pleasantries, but I realized they couldn't all be as blind as I had been. I felt out of place as I entered my office, like I was a stranger who didn't belong in this building.

My desk was just as I had left it three days earlier, blue tablets neatly piled next to the monitor. Seeing them made my blood run cold. I had been helping these monsters for so many years, but no more. I shoved the tablets to the ground and pulled my chair close to the desk. I connected my earpiece and my datapad to the console, uploading everything I had done, seen, and written in the last seventy-two hours. That familiar feeling of being watched seized me, blood rushing through my ears and my heart crawling into my throat. I knew there were cameras in the room, and I knew the Nanobots filling my veins were constantly monitoring every system I needed to survive. I had worked so hard, I didn't care anymore. I opened the files on my monitor.

Everything updated so incredibly slowly, it felt as if my skin was crawling with anticipation and fear. As the system accepted the files, a pounding knock came on my door. I looked up for just a second, but long enough to see the outline of shoes in the light under the entrance. I needed to go quicker. Adrenaline rushed through my veins as I pulled my attention back towards the task in front of me.

My hand hovered over the screen. I needed to do this. Another knock. I looked up at the door once more, but it was too late. My chest tightened and I felt my throat constricting as if an animal had wrapped itself around my neck. I stood from my desk in an effort to face whoever was at the door but was hit with a wave of dizziness. I grasped for the edge of the desk but fell to the floor, gasping and clawing for air. The office door opened slowly, lazily, and Mr. Anderson stepped towards my computer, shaking his head in dismay at my writhing form. He walked to the computer slowly, canceling the transfer with the click of a button. I tried to scream but my tongue felt as if it was choking me, my entire purpose had been erased by one tiny, insignificant motion.

Mr. Anderson stared at me with cold eyes, "It's such a tragedy that a heart attack took you so young. You had such a bright future ahead of you at Nanotech. Your parents will be devastated, but I am sure they will come to understand. Just as I hoped you would, in time. I wasn't planning to tell you these things until you were ready, but it seems like you will leave us behind with the knowledge you so desperately craved."

I watched him over me, unable to respond.

"Nanotech has doctors all over the world, treating those in need, tweaking their minds to better them. We are building an army, Aria," the cruel man went on. "My dream was to have your family by my side as Nanotech became the world power it was always meant to be, but I guess you'll miss out on that opportunity. Such a shame."

Mr. Anderson stepped over me as I took my last breath. He didn't even look back.

Author's Note

This short story was the first one I wrote in the world of Lin City. At the point of writing this, I wanted Aria to be the main character of an entire series. I love her passion for doing what she believes is right and her willingness to dive into the unknown. Obviously, Aria's untimely demise got in the way of any future I had planned for her. Even though my initial plan changed a lot as I developed Aria and the world she lived in, "The Call From Below" is still one of my favorite short stories.

"The Call from Below" originally appeared in *Otherworldly Volume 1*, an anthology hosted by Nerd Street and published by Lucy's Lantern Literature. During 2024, I was invited to share table space at conventions to introduce this book to the con-goers. The support and encouragement from the community has been amazing, and I might just make this my life's work.

Star's Story

A Family Tradition

One of our family's favorite activities when I was little was to play Story Cubes. We would take them to a restaurant and make up stories while waiting for food.

In honor of this tradition, I wrote a flash fiction story set in Lin City based on Story Cubes rolls. Maybe Star will make a cameo in other Lin City tales.

Star is a high-class resident on the eleventh level of Lin City. People throughout her level and the entire city know her very well. She is also a three-pound Pomeranian. Star's owner is the captain of the Lin City Guard, so her fame stems from a bit of nepotism.

Almost daily, Star's owner will take Star on his patrol around the upper levels of Lin City to visit guards at their posts. Because of the upper levels' altitude, the chillier temperatures affect many guards more than the temperatures in Midtown, where most of them come from. Star loves to help carry extra blankets for the newer guards.

Star loves living in Lin City, but she often wonders how much the residents really like her. Whenever Star is seen on the news with her owner, she receives endless praise. That praise rarely carries over to when Star runs into these people on her walks. They often pretend they don't even see her. Star thinks this is because people don't really like animals in Lin City. The only other pets she has ever met were a handful of noisy parakeets kept by a very rich woman on the eleventh level.

Even though Star doesn't know many other animals, she still used to have a best friend. A few years back, Star and her owner were neighbors to a reclusive old man. Star always walked to the man's apartment in the afternoon to keep him company while he worked on his puzzles. She would often eat a couple of puzzle pieces to extend their time together. Eventually, the old man began to act his age. His eyesight decreased and his hands started to shake. Like many other elderly people Star had met, the old many had to leave. This only made Star feel even lonelier.

After the old man left, Star's owner began taking her on more walks around Uptown. Star enjoyed this new activity. She finally got to see the luxury of Lin City outside her apartment. All the buildings seemed huge to Star, like shining mountains.

After a long day of walking, Star's owner would sit with Star on their plush couch, listening to the sounds of Lin City winding down for the night.

The Reboot

Author's Note

Our family has had quite a debate as to whether this story takes place in Lin City or not. I finally gave in and realized that there is a place for it in the city's secret underbelly. This story has been a very important part of my writing career. I wrote "The Reboot" in eighth grade, and it was first published through a competition with LuneSpark. I take great pride in being able to say I still enjoy reading something I wrote as an eighth grader, so I hope you enjoy this newly edited edition.

My life has been reduced to pacing. Back and forth and back and forth with tedious repetition, as if I am now hard-wired to do nothing else.

The air around me smells of soil and iron, a combination I didn't think would be as foul as it truly is. The cement walls forming the room seem to glare at me, sharp and random edges hindering my every step. There is no exit. At least, no exit besides a barred and foggy window, slightly tinted orange from what I hope is the evening sun.

How did I arrive here? When did I arrive here? The last thing I remember was… nothing. Absolutely nothing. A vast emptiness fills the place in my mind where memories should reside. My pacing around the small room quickens as I rub my chin anxiously. Is this my first memory? If every memory I have is gone, how do I know how to think or walk or speak?

And now I am sitting, my eyes open. I don't remember ever sitting; I don't even remember walking to the wall. What is going on in this place, and what do I have to do with it? I again stand up, walk to my window and slide a hand in between the bars, wiping off a streak of moisture. The condensation feels strangely sticky on my hand, like syrup or soft caramel.

I wipe my hand off on one of the cement walls and leave amber streaks that slowly roll to the ground. It feels like I shouldn't be able to see the room around me so clearly. The window is dark, but there is still a soft glow emanating from a single bulb in the ceiling.

I begin searching for some sort of escape. A door, a sliding window, a vent in the ceiling, anything to get me out of this constricting prison. The more rational part of my brain wonders if it is necessary to leave at all. I'm not hungry or tired or longing to return to a life I don't even remember. There is something in the air, though. Something urging me to leave. My brain is telling me that if I don't bolt for an exit now, I will never make it out alive.

I move away from the window and walk across the room. I weave around the jutting angles of cement that protrude from every side, but I can't reach the furthest wall. I can see it, of course, it is never more than 10 feet away. My heart pounds with rising panic as I continue walking. The wall doesn't grow any closer, but I am not about to give up this early. I can't remember anything from my former life, but I know whoever I was, I didn't give up.

As I walk, I notice more details. A black circle on the wall. Orange splashes of vibrant paint covering the light. I keep walking as the orange changes to a shade of blue and the room gets colder. I continue forward, and it grows colder until my teeth begin to grind and chatter against each other.

I rub my bare, prickly arms and legs in an effort to warm them up, but my shivering continues and the wall never closes in. Snow begins falling from the blue paint in the ceiling, leaving a dusting of clean white powder over everything. My toes feel as if they will freeze off, along with my fingers and nose. I scrape my foot on the cement beneath the snow and cry out as a drop of blood taints the white. I close my eyes in pain, but when I open them, the lights are no longer covered in paint. It's warm, and the outcroppings have ceased to hinder my path.

I breathe a sigh of relief as I turn back to look at the sticky window just 50 feet away. Had I really only walked this far? No. It's not possible. Lights dance behind the window and I pivot back. Nothing will distract me from my escape.

I focus ahead and see a large gray door. It couldn't have been there before. I would have noticed it by now. I grit my teeth with a new determination and walk towards the door. This time, as I walk, the black circle grows over the wall to my right. The circle overtakes the room, an inky blackness that covers the light and fills in the small cracks in the cement walls.

I can't even tell if I am walking towards the door anymore, or walking at all. The walls begin to undulate and writhe as if turned to jelly. Psychedelic patterns grow up the walls and make me sick just looking at them.

Stumbling around the room, I try to regain my bearings amidst the bright patterns swaying in my vision. I finally close my eyes and thank the darkness that fills them. I place my hands firmly against a wall and begin walking until my head stops spinning. Electric greens and every shade of red and pink meet my gaze when I open my eyes again, but I am far more prepared this time and recover quickly.

As I walk, the patterns slowly fade back into the slate grey walls, which return to their normal, stationary state. I feel something new and powerful pulsing through my veins. I am never turning back again, never even chancing a glance at that disgusting amber window or what horrid, glowing creatures might lurk behind it. I continue.

I start towards the door I have stared at for so long. My legs pump beneath me as I break into a frantic run. My hands form fists as I run, and I'm not slowing down. The hard cement leaves my feet red and raw, but I can't stop now.

The air grows humid as I run, muggy condensation seeping into my lungs. Soft buzzing fills the air as if an enormous insect is floating behind me. The air smells of some exquisitely divine citrus; I can nearly taste the juice on my tongue. Long vines begin growing out of small cracks in the walls, tendrils of green with thorns reaching around, searching for something. Searching for me.

The vines trap my struggling arms. I recoil from one mass of plants only to be caught by another. I shriek as thorns dig into my skin. More vines grab me with their long, winding tendrils.

I yell again, this time weaker, as I hang my head and pain throbs through my limbs and mind as if the vines have ensnared my soul. Then I feel it again. That strange energy, an urge to run, to feel the wind in my hair and on my skin as I escape this vile prison.

I bare my teeth and scream at the vines. They shudder but hold fast. I break one of my arms free and tear the thorns out of my legs. It is excruciating, but that doesn't matter. The only thing that matters is getting to that door. Even if it doesn't hold answers, it holds an escape.

With vines still clinging to my legs, I run. My hands are swimming through the air in a vain attempt to push me towards the door faster. As I free the final tendrils from my legs and arms, I am suddenly there. Tears of joy and relief spill down my cheeks as my hands reach out and touch the door.

Not just the door, but its steel handle as well. There is a piece of crisp white paper stuck to the door, something I hadn't noticed before. It holds a name in bold black letters. My name, I think. I reach for the handle and slowly push it open with a soft click, as if an unseen lock has aligned to open.

I take one last deep breath of the sweet, fruity air, and step through the door into a hallway of doors just like the one I opened, but I am no longer a person being tortured by vines and cold like all the others behind the doors filling my vision, I am someone who has escaped.

I am Natasha

Lin City's Finest

Scene 1: Arrival

Lin City was a marvel of technology. Its citizens were some of the very first to experience datapads when they were released, and many of the most brilliant minds in electronics and technology lived there. Skyscrapers reached higher than the eye could see, stretching like fingers into the sky. The possibilities were endless in the nine levels of this magnificent city.

It is precisely the magnitude of possibilities that brought me to Lin City.

I stepped off the intercity transport and out onto the gray loading platform on Level Seven, holding my med bag in one hand and a battered suitcase in the other. A crowd of people pushed past me to board the transport, and immediately overwhelmed me like a tidal wave. They all looked so important, so focused, like their sole purpose in life was to board this train.

After spending most of my life in the outer townships, the excitement of Lin City sent a shock through my nervous system. The faces, the smells, even the clothes differed completely from the mundane alternative to which I was accustomed. I glanced to one side as I pushed my way through the crowds. My attention was drawn to one of the city natives on their way to . . . somewhere important. They were covered in shimmering fabrics that rippled like golden liquid as they moved onto the train. Lin City was a collection of the most intelligent and eccentric people on the planet. Soon, I would join the ranks of the most revered.

Doctors like me never had many opportunities in the townships. I was never happy doing things the way they had always been done. Even though I graduated top of my class and a year early, no one would accept my unconventional findings. This city would change everything.

I marveled at the sights and sounds of the city as I exited the transport station. There were lights everywhere. Billboards and street signs dazzled in the evening sun. I pulled my datapad from the tattered suitcase and checked the paperwork that I had received from my Lin City sponsor. They had provided me with an apartment in Midtown. They were very supportive that way. They believed in what I was doing.

I followed the directions on my pad through two levels of Lin City. The sky became nearly invisible the farther down I went, but the warm, white streetlights illuminated the catwalks on all the lower and middle levels. It seemed unusual to see such bustling life without the presence of the sun, but the streetlamps were oddly comforting. Apartments and shops became more tightly packed together as I reached my destination. I nearly missed the entrance to my building. I was so distracted by the color of the city. After using my new identification badge to enter the building, my apartment opened with a simple keypad code. 13-5-11.

It was a modest yet sufficient apartment. There was a small dining table with two chairs, a bed, a couch, cooking equipment, and a medium-sized data screen where I could view the weekly enrichment programs broadcast throughout the city.

I laid my things out on the dining table. My med bag was comprised of tools I had acquired during my time as a student, as well as some of my own creation. I specialized in biologically engineered organisms, so many of my inventions were based on the world around me. I had an adhesive made from tree sap, a scalpel shaped like an eagle's claw, and even a pair of tweezers I modeled on scorpion pincers.

My suitcase was much less interesting. I packed a few changes of clothes, some pictures of my home township, and my sketchbooks. My sketchbooks contained drawings and detailed plans for experiments I had never been able to complete.

I felt my eyes droop as I began setting my things out around the apartment. I moved into the bathroom and surveyed myself in the mirror's reflective surface. My hair had grown unkempt in the past months as I had prepared for my move into Lin City. I would have to make an appointment to remedy this.

I brushed my teeth and changed into my sleepwear before

climbing into the heavily cushioned bed. Though my body was fatigued from travel, my mind raced well into the early hours of the morning.

This was my time.

I was exactly where I belonged.

Scene 2: Preparation

When I awoke, the morning had already come and gone. The faintest rays of sun poked into the cracks of my apartment door as I dressed and ate, beckoning me out into the city.

I decided to move to Lin City on the recommendation of my sponsor. They offered me an office space on the Eighth Level of Lin City in which to host my patients, and I simply couldn't refuse. My sponsor believed the work I was doing would make the world a better place. I was forever in their debt.

I collected my med bag after I finished eating and headed up to Level Eight. I wanted to make sure the space was suitable for my needs. The city was bustling with businesspeople and artisans. Street food stalls lined the wider part of the catwalks. I pushed past the colorful art booths and arrived in Uptown, Lin City.

The office included a small waiting room, a private office, and an extra room I could use for operations or medical studies. I could feel the excitement rising in me as I toured the space. Every room reminded me of the possibilities that awaited me. I immediately sent a message to my sponsor to thank them for their generous gift.

The only thing I needed to do now was wait for the equipment I had shipped from my home to arrive in the city. In the meantime, I started searching for potential patients.

I realized that ill people were everywhere if I looked hard enough, but it was particularly easy to find them in Lin City's lower levels. Thousands of people had come to the city just like I had, in search of opportunity, but their reality had fallen short.

I printed out a few dozen copies of my contact information and a short summary of my medical services. Because I could not afford to display my ad on any enrichment programs, I printed it on flimsy plastic and plastered it around the city. I started at the upper levels and worked my way down, using a small tub of my tree sap tack to stick my posters to the sides of buildings, catwalks, and the occasional storefront bulletin board. I got a few strange looks, but nothing I was not used to seeing already.

Eventually, I made my way down to Level Two, the lowest area open to the public. The people there would be my prime customers. None of them had enough money to seek medical help from the Carson Institute or any other established practitioners. They would come to me even if it meant having to be more experimental in their treatment.

Scene 3: A Call

It was not long before I got the first call on my datapad. I was sitting in my apartment, flipping through enrichment programs, when my datapad started vibrating on the dining table.

I rushed to pick it up and greeted the caller with the cheeriest voice I could muster, "Hello! Thank you so much for calling the office of Dr. Nev. Are you calling to schedule an appointment?"

The caller was quiet for a moment, then spoke in a hoarse voice. "Yes, I need an appointment. But no one can know I'm seeing you."

I smiled at the request, filled with anticipation. "Of course. We value your privacy. We have an appointment available one week from today, if you're willing to wait."

I heard a sigh of relief from the caller. "Yes, I can come in first thing in the morning."

"Perfect!" I said, making a note of the appointment in my datapad's calendar. "Please make sure you bring your ID and the form of payment you will be using to your appointment. We look forward to your visit! Thank you again for calling the offices of Dr. Nev."

I pushed a button on my datapad to end the call and practically leaped from the table, sending my chair crashing to the floor behind me. I had my first patient!

Scene 4: Patient 01

The next few days were busy. Between establishing my new office and adjusting to life in Lin City, I was swamped. One thing that was a welcome adjustment was the food. The cuisine in the city was a blend of flavors from cultures around the world. Every new food I tried was better than the last.

Adapting to the weather in Lin City, though, proved quite the challenge. It seemed to change with every level. When I first inspected my office on the Eighth Level, I was surprised by the chill of the breeze, but in the lower levels, it was much warmer. I knew logically that this was caused by the elevation of the upper levels, but the science seemed almost magical. Sometimes it felt as if the different levels of Lin City were on entirely different planets.

When it came time to see Patient 01, my office was ready. I had the movers place everything exactly where I needed it: desk and chairs in the lobby, two sterile examination tables, and a large data screen for my private office.

I had left my office door open for the patient, and practically sprinted to greet him as he entered. Patient 01 scuttled in quickly like a tiny mouse looking around the room to check for traps. I ushered the patient to the examination table and sat across from him. I started my recording device and set it on the desk.

"Hello. Could you say your name for the recording, and please list any symptoms you've been experiencing?"

Patient 01 nodded and spoke, voice quiet. "My name is Jay Ward. I have a cough, have had a cough for the past few weeks. Also, a slight fever, and this."

The patient rolled up a sleeve on his stained work shirt to

reveal a large rash covering his arm. It appeared to continue up the arm, past where I could see.

I nodded and gestured for the patient to sit at the examination table. "Based on the symptoms you describe, it seems like you have a bacterial infection. This is most likely caused by poor nutrition and proximity to others with the same infection." I tried to calm my voice, but I was excited to diagnose my first patient.

I ran my nitrile-covered hand over the rash. It was warm, and had raised nodules filled with fluid. I had seen infections like this one in the townships, mostly among the poorest civilians.

"I will be able to help you, but I require payment upfront," I said, removing one of my gloves and producing a small scanner from a drawer next to me.

The patient was hesitant, but—with a glance at the swollen rash on his arm—pulled an old datapad from his back pocket. I scanned the code on the datapad screen and, once the transaction was approved, set the scanner aside to prepare for treatment.

I enjoyed working with this patient much more than my previous few in my experiments. I didn't struggle nearly as much to sedate the human patient as I did the small rodents I usually worked with.

Of course, there was no genuine need for an operation in this case. I probably could have prescribed a bottle of chewable tablets that would've cleared the rash in a week, but this patient had a nobler purpose than returning to his life in the dirt of Downtown.

The offering of Patient 01, though unchosen by him, would serve as a gateway to improved research. Perhaps someday I would use what I had harvested to save another dozen lives, and I only needed to sacrifice one.

The entire office smelled like cleaning solution once I had completed the operation, something I barely noticed until I removed my mask. I surveyed my newly filled display cabinets in the back of my office. If I had new specimens to study, my patient's sacrifice would be justified.

As I closed the office for the night, my upcoming research filled me with excitement. I would build a life for myself in Lin City, no matter what it took.

Scene 5: Collecting

I had a few days until my next patient would arrive at my office, so I made plans to visit my sponsor's collection outside the city. Their menagerie was one of the most exotic I had come across. It included countless nearly extinct specimens. I, of course, had free range in the collection, to see and take whatever I desired. I tried to avoid the reptiles; scales were not something I often used in my work. On this trip, I had a very specific item in mind.

Before departing for the collection, I had received a private communication from Patient 02 requesting a personalized service.

The patient was suffering from extreme vision loss, and nothing seemed to slow the degeneration. Though I could not yet reverse the effects of aging, there were treatments I could apply to improve one's eyesight.

I finished my trip with a visit to the felis catus enclosure, where I was able to find just the thing Patient 02 required. My sponsor made sure I was well-prepared, even for the strangest of procedures.

Scene 6: Patient 02

Patient 02 arrived on time for her appointment, just a few hours after my return from the collection, and she was not what I was expecting. This patient had freshly trimmed hair and wore fine robes. Her gold and silver jewelry shimmered in the fluorescent light as she stepped in. Needless to say, I was not worried about my compensation for this appointment.

"Hello. Doctor Nev, I presume?" Patient 02 asked, glancing around the compact office before holding out their hand for me to shake. "My name is Lyann Holland."

I shook her hand before responding. "You presume correctly. I received your communication about the work you require. If you have payment for me, we can begin."

Patient 02 nodded and produced an envelope. Almost no one in Lin City used physical currency, but the nature of this procedure required extreme confidentiality, and this method of payment ensured that no record of it would leave my office. Other evidence of the procedure would be more obvious, but wouldn't be traced back to me.

After stowing the payment in one of my desk drawers, I escorted the patient to the operating room. Once she had settled onto the examination table, I showed her what I would be using. The striking color of the feline eyes I had procured impressed the patient. She even commented on how the bright yellow would match her outfits. Though the small talk brought me little joy, I was excited to see my patient so filled with anticipation regarding my ideas.

Once the procedure was more formally agreed upon, I administered the anesthesia and collected my newly sterilized tools.

I began with my scalpel, and made small incisions around the existing eyes. People in the townships called me barbaric for wanting to help people like this. Looking into Patient 02's cloudy eyes, I thought it quite barbaric to let my fellow humans suffer when I could ease their pain.

I wasn't able to find suitable feline eyes to match the size of human eyes, so the skin had to be slightly stretched after I finished the implantation stage. It would not look perfect, but the skin would heal as the eyes did. Once the donor eyes were properly accepted, I bandaged the patients' eyes to prepare them for healing.

An attendant waited outside my office to collect the patient, so I didn't need to worry about my project being properly taken care of. As Patient 02 stirred awake, I handed her off to the attendant, and also handed her a file drive filled with reading material, mostly written by myself, about the procedure and the healing process. I always wanted my patients to leave well-informed.

After I made sure Patient 02 had left the building, I once again locked my office door. It was very important to me that no one interrupt my cleaning, especially when dealing with specimens as fragile as human eyes.

I placed the discarded spheres into a container on my display shelves. I might've been able to replace the eye lens and lessen some vision issues when given time, but I couldn't guarantee perfect clarity for future recipients.

Scene 7: Experimental

It was a few more days before I had a procedure of any interest. Though my cases of specimens grew a bit, I was bored with the diseases of Lin City. I wanted to feel challenged, as I had with the feline eyes. I had come to Lin City to experiment and change the world, but all I was doing was treating the barking coughs and fevers that now consumed my every waking moment. My sponsor had warned me against experimenting too frequently, but I needed to practice my craft. I started calling the larger medical facilities and asking, begging, for contact information for any patients that they were forced to turn away because they were at capacity. Somewhat unsurprisingly, they refused.

It was a couple of weeks after my first procedure in Lin City when I heard a knock. I sat in my office lobby, flipping through one of my most recent sketchbooks. I looked up, startled. I wasn't expecting any patients that day.

I walked to the office door tentatively and peaked through the small view hole near its center. A hooded figure stood on the other side of the door, hands fidgeting with a datapad.

I opened the door and stuck my head through, sizing up the stranger.

"My apologies. I don't have any openings for patients today. Call ahead if you want an appointment."

I tried to close the door, but the man pushed his way into my office and shoved his datapad into my hands. I stepped back, shocked.

"Excuse me, you need to leave. I am truly sorry, but there are no appointments available today!" I tried to push the figure back outside, but he held his ground and pushed the datapad toward me again.

I finally looked down at the datapad and read the words that were typed into the display.

Hello. My name is Cam Avery, I have never possessed the ability to speak. You can help me, and I have payment.

I raised an eyebrow and looked up at the figure. "Well, I appreciate your directness. Please, sit."

I gestured to a set of chairs facing each other and sat, pointing to the chair across from me. The figure sat, pulled his datapad from my hands, and placed it in front of him. He updated the screen on his datapad, preparing to type for our conversation.

My sketchbook was still open on my desk, and I saw him glance at the page that I had been investigating. I had always been fascinated with the evolution of mimic birds, some of which could even recreate human speech.

Before I could speak again, the patient removed his hood and tapped the open sketchbook. He looked back at me with large, insistent brown eyes.

I shook my head in response. "I have not yet tested any part of that procedure. Performing it now would be completely irresponsible and immensely dangerous."

He typed something quickly on his datapad before sliding it toward me again.

I will give you any payment you require. If the procedure is unsuccessful, I will ensure there is no possibility of it being traced back to you.

I sighed, but when he showed me the transfer waiting in his account, I made up my mind.

"Very well. I will perform the procedure. I must collect the proper specimens for you outside of the city. Please wait in my office until I return this afternoon. If anyone finds out about this operation, it will be over for both of us." I stated, watching my newest patient grin and lean back in his chair, nodding in agreement with what I had said.

I quickly pulled my jacket off the wall and rushed into the bustling streets of Lin City. The transport was packed as I made my way toward the collection. This was the most reckless and irresponsible procedure for which I had ever prepared. Adrenaline rushed through my veins as the transport shuddered to a halt.

As usual, my sponsor was not at the collection when I arrived. I let myself into the aviary and walked through the bizarre assemblage of birds. Some birds blotted out the sun with their vast wings as they flew overhead; others were small enough to perch on the tip of my thumb. Eventually, I found what I was looking for.

The magpie is a sleek bird known for its white and black feathering and its human-like traits. The bird was exactly what I had in mind for my patient. I administered a lethal dose of medication to the beautiful creature via a small syringe I always kept in my coat pocket. The magpie fell limp in my hand. I quickly thanked the bird for its sacrifice before placing it into a sterile bag and leaving the aviary.

I returned to my office with the specimen to find Patient 21 perched on the edge of my desk, working on his datapad. I hung my coat back up on its hook and began sterilizing my equipment for the operation.

I placed a fresh plastic cover over the operating bed and

washed the new specimen with a cocktail of cleaning products before placing it carefully on the table next to my tools. Patient 21 observed my preparations and inspected the avian specimen carefully. After preparing the room, Patient 21 eagerly lay down on the operating bed. I administered the anesthetic and began one of my most ambitious procedures.

The challenge of the procedure, in part, was the considerable size difference between a magpie and a human. When I inspected the patient's voice box, I quickly discovered that he had been born with laryngeal atresia, a condition which affects the formation of the larynx. I was able to use both the larynx and the syrinx from the bird, along with some human tissue I had collected from previous patients, to compensate for the missing portions.

I slaved for hours over the operating table, making miniscule adjustments with my forceps until everything sat perfectly in the cavity I had opened. I finished the procedure by sewing two rows of stitches along the incisions, careful not to puncture the donated specimens. The anesthetic wore off just a few minutes after I finished the procedure. Though disoriented at first, the patient soon began trying to speak.

"No, you can't speak yet. You must wait for your body to fully accept the transplants. I don't even know if this operation will be successful." I said, leaning back in my chair and removing my surgical mask.

The patient nodded, clearly understanding what I had said.

I had the man stay for a few hours after I had completed the operation, monitoring his vitals as I instructed him on the proper way to care for and utilize his new vocal tools. When he was finally ready to leave, I let out a sigh of relief I had been holding in for longer than I realized.

It took me some time to clean my operating room after my patient had left. The number of resources I had used for the procedure was staggering, but I had also received enough compensation to fund my life in Lin City for the next several weeks.

Scene 8: Consequences

The day following the procedure on Patient 21, I went shopping. Coming from a township, the thrill of shopping in Uptown Lin City was unmatched. Countless jewelers and an upscale clothing store beckoned me in with glittering stones and vibrant fabrics. You could practically smell the wealth on everyone in Uptown.

After surveying my options, I decided on a men's clothing store filled with fine suits and shiny time pieces. The attendees were a pair of men, both eager to outfit me with their most expensive pieces.

Once I had considered the choices, I settled on a finely woven gray suit and an expensive looking watch. There were many flashier outfits that fit the general aesthetics of Lin City, but I thought a doctor should remain more reserved.

I left the shop feeling refreshed and recovered from the long operation the day before. I decided to take another visit to my office. I liked to finish off my evenings with some new research, but tonight was different.

When I reached the large building, my office was located in, I noticed more security personnel surveying the area than usual. I tried to ignore them as I scanned my identification badge. There was no way they could've found out anything about my experiments, right?

My stomach sank as I approached my office. A set of three city guards stood in front of my office. They were waiting for me. The guards saw me, and I knew it was over; there was no point in resisting now. One of the guards twisted my arms behind me and placed a set of magnetic cuffs around my wrists. I could feel questions rising from my mind, but I kept my mouth shut. Anything I said would just make my treatment worse.

Finally, as I was escorted away from my office, the guard to my left told me the reason for my arrest.

"Mari Nev. In accordance with Lin City code 3998, Water Conservation Act 4, you are under arrest for excessive overuse of water resources." The guard stated, completely monotone.

I tripped over my own feet as I processed what the guard had said. "Wait, what?"

The guard sighed and began reading the charge again. I shushed him quickly and stared at all of the guards in shock.

"You're arresting me for water?" I yelled, struggling against the cuffs as I was led to a Lin City guard station.

I had expected to face consequences for my medical practices eventually, but for water? None of the guards responded to my question.

The guard leading me scanned a special card on the door and pulled me toward an elevator at the back of the station. They pressed the button for level one and turned to me, finally responding to my question.

"As you most likely know from the news enrichment programs, Lin City is experiencing an extreme drought. Your excessive water use was completely irresponsible," they stated, still as serious as ever.

The elevator dinged as we reached the lowest level of Lin City. The doors slid open smoothly, and I was hit by a gust of hot, damp air. This level of the city must have been underground, evidenced by the poor circulation of air.

This was an entirely different world from the shining city above. It was dark, dank, and dirty. The place was filled with people in grimy uniforms and stray animals that had slipped between cracked walls and metal gates. Malnourished and flea-ridden dogs barked at me as I approached, and no one bothered to quiet them.

I was pulled by the cuff of my new suit toward a large gate with a sign that read: Patient Input. Before we got too far through the gates, someone handed me a datapad.

"You get one call. Make it count."

I nodded in response to the voice whose face I never saw and began typing my sponsor's identification number into the pin pad. The call rang through, but there was no answer. I would have to leave a message for them without even knowing if they would get it. I turned my face away from as many guards as I could before I spoke, keeping my voice low.

"This is Mari Nev. I have been arrested for excessive water use. Please retrieve my things from my office." I tried not to let my voice shake as I finished my message. No point in showing unnecessary weakness.

One guard took the datapad from my hands and continued shuffling me forward. I was still in shock as the guards stripped me of my belongings. How could this have happened? I was so careful about hiding my work that I neglected the simplest rules of life in Lin City. In my defense, I had no idea that the penalty for not conserving water could be this severe.

The guards pushed me through rows of sanitation tanks and sprays before I was given a prison work uniform. One guard spoke to me as I dressed myself.

"For the crime of not following Lin City code 3998, Water Conservation Act 4, you have been hereby sentenced to six months' confinement and work detail without trial. If we are presented with sufficient evidence by a contact of your choice that you are, in fact, not guilty of this crime, we will release you immediately."

Once the guard had finished talking, the other turned to glare at me like I had killed someone! I had, of course, but they didn't know that.

I adjusted the various elastic straps on the gray uniform when another, more armored, guard led me through the labyrinth of cell blocks that filled Lin City's First Level. Each cell had three cement walls, and one wall constructed from a shimmering blue shield of some sort. The blue wall faced into the hallway and was nearly transparent, making it easy for guards to monitor prisoners. It also made it easier for prisoners to see me as I walked by.

Every way I turned, I was met with bodies wearing the same gray jumpsuit I now sported. I wondered how many of them were incarcerated on charges equally as idiotic as those I faced.

The guard scanned a keycard on a reader next to an empty cell near the end of the hallway. He gestured for me to enter. I could've sworn I saw the tiniest grin trace his lips.

I stepped into the cell and, as the shield closed behind me, my handcuffs clattered to the ground. I quickly wiped away the beads of sweat that had formed on my forehead from the trek to my cell. I assumed that dragging the prisoners around the cell blocks acted as an intimidation tactic to discourage any attempts at escape.

I heard the guard shuffling away behind me and took a quick scan of my surroundings. It was closer to the cells shown in enrichment dramas than I had imagined. Perhaps they used a retired cell for filming. On one wall, a slab of metal folded up against the wall. When lowered to a horizontal position, the cold surface acted as a bed. On the other wall, there was a similarly hinged table slab and two stools. A short commode sat in the back corner.

I pulled one of the stools down from the wall and sat, staring out into the hallway. The shields cast a bright eerie glow throughout the entire building, making it unnecessary for any extra lighting.

The man in the cell across from me looked older than me, maybe in his late thirties, and he had a scruffy beard that covered much of his lower face and neck. I tried to get his attention, but he was deeply engrossed in the datapad he held in front of him. I assumed that datapads the Lin City guard gave out to prisoners were stripped clean, and I didn't have nearly enough electronics know-how to get anything to the outside world. I would simply have to accept my fate and hope my sponsor was able to save some of my specimens before my office was torn apart by conservation investigators.

Scene 9: Finished

I rotted in that cell for weeks. Some of the other prisoners I met during work details or meals had been locked in those dehumanizing cells for years, with only the occasional stray dog as a companion. I didn't understand how they lived through it. I didn't think I would ever adjust to my new life. But life wasn't hard only on the prisoners. This must have been the lowest duty for security personnel, too. The guards weren't well.

My experiments continued when, after releasing our shields for marching toward our work detail, a guard began coughing blood. Then vomiting. Then he collapsed outside my cell door.

The other prisoners screamed for help. I stepped out of my cell and over his twitching body.

"Seizure onset. I've seen this before," I said.

The guard at the end of the corridor ran. He never came back.

"What's happening to him?" asked the man from the cell across from me.

I smiled. "Something treatable. Maybe. But he'll need a new liver." I turned to the prisoner, "Tell me. What's your blood type?"

He froze.

I glanced at the spork from last night's dinner sitting in my cell. Cheap polymer. Flexible. I could work with that.

Author's Note

After writing "A Call from Below," I knew I needed to provide some backstory for Dr. Nev, and I knew I wanted it to be creepy. I was finally motivated to write his story when my mentor, Jeri Shephard, contacted me about Otherworldy Volume Two. After debuting Macie in volume one, it only felt right. This is definitely my most gory Lin City story, but it's also my favorite.

This short story was originally published in Otherworldly Volume Two by Lucy Lantern Literature, sponsored by Nerd Street.

About the Author

Ivy Ru is a high school and college student living in Minnesota, but she is also your new favorite author! Ivy has been writing for as long as she can remember, her first short stories being about her imaginary little sister, Sinnamon. Now, Ivy has moved on from (very) realistic fiction to suspense and sci-fi. Ivy loves that she can say writing is her job and hopes that she will be able to continue to do so for many years to come. When Ivy's not writing, she enjoys playing the harp, drums, and piano, as well as practicing multiple dance styles.

If you want to get updates on all of Ivy's publications, adventures, and her current favorites from the local animal shelter, please subscribe to her newsletter!

www.IvyRuWrites.com/witb

Acknowlegements

Jeri Shepherd, for inviting me into the world of writing and being my mentor throughout this entire process. I hope we have many more productive years together!

My parents, for driving me to conventions and making sure I was actually working and not just scrolling Pinterest.

The Working Writers Mastermind, for acting as a creative escape from my everyday life and inspiring me to write in every free moment.

Teresa Moran, for occupying my mother and giving me much needed feedback.

My family, for supporting me and buying my books even though we're related. I ask for nothing in return for my kind acknowledgements, except maybe a nice review on the platform of your choice.

Whispers in the Blue

Ivy Ru's first novel! This story takes place in Lin City, right after Aria's story.

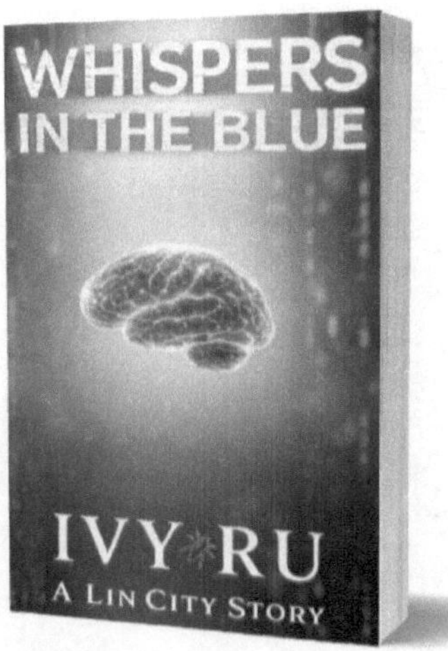

**Get your signed copy at
www.IvyRuWrites.com**

Otherworldly Volumes 1 and 2

Diverse genre-fiction authors have come together to bring you short stories exploring old, new, yet-to-come, and imagined worlds.

Purchasing Information at
www.IvyRuWrites.com

Anthology of the Damned

Three volumes of scary stories to share around the campfire. Ivy's story in *Library of Madness* is a different take on a girls' trip Up North.

Twisted Yultide

Thirteen grinchy tales to read by the fire as you watch for Krampus! Special edition hardcover and softcovers available at www.IvyRuWrites.com